MW01014579

For Isabel

First published by Éditions Sarbacane as *Le Grand Jour d'Eric*
Copyright © 2013 Éditions Sarbacane, Paris

First English edition copyright © 2014 by VeloPress

All rights reserved. Printed in Malaysia.

No part of this book may be reproduced, stored in a retrieval system, or transmitted, in any
form or by any means, electronic or photocopy or otherwise, without the prior written permis-
sion of the publisher except in the case of brief quotations within critical articles and reviews.

VeloPress
3002 Sterling Circle, Suite 100
Boulder, Colorado 80301-2338 USA
(303) 440-0601 • Fax (303) 444-6788 • E-mail velopress@competitorgroup.com
Distributed in the United States and Canada by Ingram Publisher Services

A Cataloging-in-Publication record for this book is available from the Library of Congress.
ISBN 978-1-937715-23-6

For information on purchasing VeloPress books, please call (800) 811-4210, ext. 2138,
or visit www.velopress.com.

This paper meets the requirements of ANSI/NISO Z39.48-1992 (Permanence of Paper).

14 15 16 / 10 9 8 7 6 5 4 3 2 1

ROD WATERS

ERIC'S BIG DAY

A BICYCLE RACE UNLIKE ANY OTHER

VELO press

Boulder, Colorado

It was a big day for Eric. It was the day of the Bike Race
with its colorful jerseys and flag-waving crowds.

"It finishes here in my town," said Eric's friend Emily
when she phoned him that morning. "Come and watch it
with me, and we'll find out who wins!"

"Wonderful!" replied Eric. "I'll come over at once."
And he went off to hunt for his shoes.

Emily always loved to see Eric. "We could have a nice picnic!" she thought when she saw the fine weather, then wondered just what they could take.

So she looked in her cupboard. She had cheese and tomatoes to put in the sandwiches, rosy red apples, and a bottle of pop. "Lovely!" she thought when she finished packing her picnic basket. And then she sat down to wait with her book.

Eric packed his essentials. He had no time to lose.
"Splendid!" he said as he looked in his bag.

"Two tires and a compass, a first-aid kit, some soft
caramels, and my balloon. But what I need most …"
he remembered suddenly,

"… are Emily's FLOWERS!"

And he squeezed them in on top. "Time to go!"
thought Eric as he climbed onto his bike.

And off he went.

The sun shone, the sky was an infinite blue, and Emily's flowers blew in the wind. Then suddenly a cyclist flew past with a yell. *Whooooosh—splash!* Eric looked up, and the rider was gone.

He'd gone over the bridge and fallen into the river. "I s-s-slipped," he spluttered as he bobbed up and down.

"What you need," announced Eric as he looked into his bag, "are these!" And, tying his tires into a rope, he fished the poor cyclist out.

"Quick!" Eric said. "Follow me!" And off they went.

Eric rode faster; he didn't want to be late. As he rounded a corner, he saw a road sign. Its directions were broken and twisted, and beneath it a cyclist looked as sad as can be.

"I'm lost!" sobbed the cyclist as he looked for his handkerchief.

"So I see," pondered Eric as he looked down the road. "What you need," he said, "is this!" and he pulled out his compass to see where to go.

"Quick!" Eric said. "Follow me!" And off they went.

The bees buzzed, and the warm air tugged at the petals on Emily's flowers. Just then, a cyclist swept past with a wave. But then … *hissss* went his tire, and the cyclist stopped.

"I have a flat tire!" he groaned as he reached for his pump.

"Now what you need is a small pair of these!" declared Eric in triumph. He took two bandages from his first-aid kit and stuck them on over the hole.

"Quick!" said Eric. "Emily's waiting!"
And off they went.

The day was getting hot, and they were pleased when the road turned under some trees. But there in a ditch stood a cyclist holding his bike and its wheel.

"Ummm … it fell off," confessed the cyclist, just a little embarrassed.

"Then I think what you need," said Eric as he opened his bag, "are a couple of these!" And he whipped out some caramels to stick the wheel back on.

"Quick!" said Eric. "Follow me!" And off they went.

Their wheels hummed, the birds sang, and Emily's flowers were still losing their petals when suddenly there on the hill was a cyclist, riding so slowly it looked like he'd stopped!

"I'm exhausted," he wheezed, and then promptly fell over.

"What you need," puffed Eric, blowing up his balloon, "is a large one of these!" And he tied it onto the cyclist's jersey, who then floated up over the hill.

"Quick!" Eric gasped. "Follow me!" And off they went.

Then the last petal was gone. Eric's knees hurt, and his legs ached, but just ahead was Emily's town.

"What I need," panted Eric, "is not to be late!" And pedaling faster, they reached the first streets. People stood on the roadside and leaned out of windows to give them a cheer. "You can do it!" they yelled from high on their balconies as the bikes whistled past.

"I must not be late," whispered Eric as he thought of Emily still waiting. And off they went.

So quickly did Eric speed through the streets that he shot under a banner and into a big group of reporters.

BANG! Notebooks and cameras flew high in the air.

As Eric sat on the road with his bag in front of him, his pitiful flowers were now plain to see.

"What I need," said Eric quietly as his eyes filled with tears … but before he could finish, someone reached for his hand.

"Follow me," said a tall lady in a fancy dress.
And off they went.

At first, all Eric heard were the cheers, and all he saw were the camera flashes. Then out from the crowd stepped the mayor.

"You have WON the Bike Race!" the mayor said heartily in a booming voice. He presented Eric with some magnificent flowers.

"Hooray!" Eric cried, and the crowds loudly cheered him. But on seeing the time, he remembered his friend. "What I need," he said anxiously, "is my bike!"

And off he went.

Emily sat on the wall beside her house and began to cry.
She'd waited and waited, but Eric had not come. Then a
bicycle bell jingled. Turning, she saw an enormous
bouquet.

"Hello, Emily, these flowers are for you!" came Eric's
voice from behind them, and Emily laughed as she walked
over to give him a hug. He began to explain, but Emily
picked up her basket.

"What we need," she said with a smile, "is this PICNIC!"

"Follow me," said Emily. And off they went.

 THE END